NEW BOOKS FOR NEW READERS

Phyllis MacAdam, *General Editor*

YO-ABK-589

Kentucky Home Place

Lee A. Dew

The University Press of Kentucky

Publication of this volume was made possible in part by a grant from the National Endowment for the Humanities.

Scholarly publisher for the Commonwealth,
serving Bellarmine College, Berea College, Centre
College of Kentucky, Eastern Kentucky University,
The Filson Club Historical Society, Georgetown College,
Kentucky Historical Society, Kentucky State University,
Morehead State University, Murray State University,
Northern Kentucky University, Transylvania University,
University of Kentucky, University of Louisville,
and Western Kentucky University.

Editorial and Sales Offices: The University Press of Kentucky
663 South Limestone Street, Lexington, Kentucky 40508-4008

03 02 01 00 99   5 4 3 2 1

Cover illustration from *Illustrated Atlas of the
Upper Ohio River Valley*, 1877.

Library of Congress Cataloging-in-Publication Data

Dew, Lee. A.
    Kentucky home place / Lee A. Dew.
        p.   cm. — (New books for new readers)
    ISBN 0-8131-0911-6 (pbk. : alk. paper)
    1. Farm life—Kentucky—History—Fiction. 2. Family—
Kentucky—History—Fiction. 3. Readers for new literates.
I. Title. II. Series.
PE1126.A4D49   1999
428.6'2—dc21   98-49552

Contents

Foreword

The Kentucky Humanities Council began New Books for New Readers because Kentucky's adult literacy students want books that recognize their intelligence and experience while meeting their need for simplicity in writing. The first ten titles in the New Books for New Readers series have helped many adult students open the window on the wonderful world of literacy. At the same time, these New Books, with their plain language and compelling stories of Kentucky history and culture, have found a wider audience among accomplished readers of all ages who recognize a good read when they see one. As we publish the eleventh book, we thank our authors and our readers, who together have proved that New Books and the humanities are for everyone.

This volume was made possible by a gift from Martin F. Schmidt and the Martin F. Schmidt/Kate Schmidt Moninger Fund and by alumni of the Board of Directors of the Kentucky Humanities Council: Michael C.C. Adams, A.D. Albright, Philip Alperson, Philip P. Ardery, Andrew Baskin, Ina Brown Bond, George Street Boone, Jeanette M. Cawood, Madge Chesnut, John R. Combs, Nancy DeMartra, Nancy Forderhase, Jo Anne Gabbard, Janice C. Gevedon, George C. Herring, David D. Lee, Robert H. Miller, M. Janice Murphy, Paul Oberst, Josephine Richardson, Samuel Robinson and the Lincoln Foundation, Virginia Stallings, Richard Taylor, Marianne Walker, and Edwin T. Weiss.

We are grateful for the advice and support provided to us by the University Press of Kentucky and for the cosponsorship of the Kentucky Department for Libraries and Archives. The Kentucky Humanities Council thanks all of our friends and supporters who for the past ten years have shared our commitment to the important role that reading books plays in the lives of the people of our Commonwealth.

Virginia G. Smith, Executive Director

Kentucky Humanities Council

Acknowledgments

Many people deserve a hearty vote of thanks for making this book possible. First of all, my uncles, Earl Groff and Jim Devine, on whose farms I was privileged to experience the last years of horse-powered agriculture, and the Lacy family, my Uncle Earl's tenants, who taught me how the machines worked and let me drive the teams.

The Kentucky Humanities Council and The University Press of Kentucky deserve kudos for making this entire project possible, and a special word of thanks goes to Phyllis MacAdam, coordinator of the New Books for New Readers project, who was the best editor and general cheerleader that any author could want. She helped me beyond measure to understand the special needs of this project in terms of writing style and "voice."

Of course, the people who really made it happen are the people for whom the book was written—the new readers and their tutors in the literacy program at Longfellow Education Center, Owensboro, Kentucky, who read and commented upon every line of the text and offered many suggestions for its improvement. Thanks to students Charles Mattingly, Guy Cox, Curtis Lyons, and Tim Wilhite, and their tutors Glenda Rone, Louise Wethington, Theresa Thompson, and Peggy Hill. Thanks also to Volunteer Services Coordinator Sharon Hill, her administrative assistant, Tina Bernard Tague, and the AmeriCorp-Vista volunteers who arranged our visits and put everyone at ease. We worked hard and had a fine time.

All illustrations courtesy of Audio-Visual Archives,
Special Collections and Archives, University of Kentucky Libraries.

1

Young Jeff's World

1816

Our log cabin stands on a wooded hill. Off to the west about 300 yards is the Green River of Kentucky. We are on the high side of the river. There is a good bank so that floods will not reach us. The lowlands across the river flood a lot, but we are always high and dry.

Two big white oaks stand in front of our cabin, giving shade and breeze on even the hottest days. Lots of folks cut down the trees close to their cabins for firewood, but my Pa wanted the shade. He picked this spot partly because of these two big old trees.

Pa built the cabin in the summer of 1799 when he and Ma and my Uncle Jim and Aunt Becky moved to the Green River country from Virginia. They came on foot and horseback through the Cumberland Gap along the pioneer trail. When they found the land they wanted, they marked it. Pa picked out a place that had three things: lots of tall timber, good sloping land with no swamps, and good water. Trees grow best on good land, and the rotted leaves make rich soil. Pa knew it was a fine place for a farm.

He made sure they had a good, legal deed to their land. A lot of the people who came to Kentucky got cheated out of land if they didn't have good deeds. Ma and Pa named their farm The Home Place, and that's what it is to me.

My name is Jeff Boyd. It's really Thomas Jefferson Boyd. I was born in 1800, one year after my folks settled here on the Green River. It was also the year Mr. Thomas Jefferson got elected the third president of the United States. He was a Virginia farmer like my folks. They thought he was a great man.

We have a good life here. Our log cabin is not big, but it is strong, and it fills our needs. Pa and Uncle Jim chose tulip poplar logs for the cabin because they don't rot and insects don't get into them so bad.

A stream flows by our hill. It has lots of flat sandstone, so we have stone steps and a stone base under the logs to keep them from rotting. We can also store things under the cabin where it is dry.

Our chimney is built from the same river sandstone. At first we had a chimney made of twigs plastered with clay. That chimney broke apart in the big earthquake of 1811. Early in the morning of December 16, 1811, the ground began to shake something awful. We ran outside and watched that old chimney just fall away from the cabin. The quakes continued for weeks. Without a chimney we couldn't build a fire. It was so cold that winter, and we didn't have any heat. We tried to keep a little fire in the fireplace for cooking. It would have been too dangerous to have a big fire. We almost froze that winter, but we were lucky. It could have been worse. Nobody got hurt, and our new barn was not damaged.

That spring Pa decided to build a strong stone chimney. We got the stones from the creek, but they needed cement to hold them together. To make the cement Pa got mussel shells at the river and heated them in a fire. When they were hot, he smashed them into powder. He mixed the powder with water and sand to make a strong cement for the chimney. Now we can build a roaring fire and stay good and warm during winter.

Inside, our cabin has one big square room about 16 feet by 16 feet, with the fireplace along one side. The fireplace is wide enough to take four-foot logs with lots of room left over. We move the logs from one side to the other so we can clean out the ashes and still keep a fire all night in the winter. Fire is so hard to start with flint and steel that we never want it to go out. It's a big job to cut enough wood to keep the fire going, but it's worth it not to have to start a new one.

Inside the cabin we have some furniture made from wood. Ma and Pa have a rope bed made with a wooden frame with ropes tied across it to hold the cornshuck mattress. The ropes have to be made tight from time to time because they sag. We say "sleep tight" when the ropes are tight and the bed is most comfortable.

My brother and sister and I sleep up in a loft under the roof. My brother John is two years older than me. My sister Katie is four years younger. I'm 16 now, and my brother John is 18. He is planning to leave home and go west to the Missouri Territory where land is cheaper. Some folks down-river are moving to Missouri next spring. John may go with them. They have a girl he is sweet on, I think.

I'm big enough to do a man's work on the farm, so it's all

right with the family if John leaves. The hardest work is already done, building the cabin and fences and clearing the first fields. Still, there is always plenty of work to do.

After Pa and Ma built the cabin, they needed to make some space for crops. They began the farm by killing many of the trees so that sunlight could get down to the ground. They cut through the bark into the wood all around the tree to kill it. We call this "girdling" the trees. Then they poked holes in the ground with a pointed stick and put in corn and bean seeds. This was the way they raised their first crops.

After a few years they cut down the dead trees and dug up the stumps. Then they had a field. It had to be worked with a plow to break up the ground. It also had to be weeded. Weeds and grass got started in the sunlight just like the crops did. It's too bad we can't grow the crops we want without having to fight weeds and grass. I guess nothing in life comes without work.

Every year they girdle more trees and cut some down for logs and fence rails. After a few years we had several acres cleared. Now we have lots of crop land.

We have a problem with deer coming into the fields. They are big pests because they eat our crops. We had to build rail fences up about six feet high to keep them out. Pa and Uncle Jim cut oak trees and split the trunks into rails to make the fences. We used flat foundation stones to keep the rails off the ground so they won't rot. Our fences will last for many years. As we expand our fields, we have to keep building more fences.

We also have a fence around the pasture where we keep the

cow. The cow is Ma's pride and joy. Ma and Pa brought her with them from Virginia when she was just a calf. Now that she is old, she is like a family pet. We bred her to a neighbor's bull, and we have two young cows, so we will have plenty of milk and cheese.

We trade our milk to Aunt Becky in return for her weaving. She has a loom and likes to make cloth. Ma grows some flax, and Aunt Becky weaves it into cloth for us. Ma then makes us britches and coats out of the linen cloth. She also grows a little cotton and spins some thread so Aunt Becky can weave cotton cloth for shirts and dresses.

Around here, we swap work and whatever we have. We all depend on each other because nobody can raise or make everything they need. We have to work together building cabins because the logs are much too heavy to handle without a lot of help. That's just the way life is here in Kentucky. It's "United we stand, divided we fall," as people say around here.

Most of our farm is still in woods. There are several kinds of oak trees, especially white and black oaks, poplars, chestnuts, and walnuts. These trees provide a good place to hunt squirrels when we are in the mood for a big pot of burgoo. Burgoo is a stew we make out of meat and vegetables.

We eat a lot of wild food. We gather walnuts, hickory nuts, wild grapes, persimmons, and sweet pawpaws in the fall. Summer brings wild cherries, plums, and blackberries. In the spring we gather wild greens for the pot. We have poke, dock, lamb's quarters, sheep sorrel, and dandelions. Ma makes us eat greens to thin our blood after the winter. She says they are healthy. I would rather have corn bread and bacon—that's my favorite.

One of the best times of the year is in the early winter when we gather honey. Pa is good at tracking bees. He can always find a bee tree. He marks the tree in the summer when the bees are active. Then, when the weather starts to get cold, we rob the tree to get the honey. We never take it all, because the bees have to live too. We want them to make more honey for the next year.

We use honey as our sweetening all year. We also use the beeswax. We make candles for light and use the wax on our saw blades to make them cut smoother. We also rub beeswax on all sorts of leather things, such as boots and harnesses, to keep the leather from drying out and cracking.

The Green River has lots of fish, and it is great fun to go fishing. I like to fish with a pole. We have fish hooks that Pa brought from Virginia. Now that I am old enough, I can use them. I am proud when I can catch enough fish for the whole family for supper. Ma coats the fish with corn meal and fries them in hot lard. She always fries up a bunch of doughballs made with corn meal and chopped onion to go with the fish. We call them "hush puppies," because the dogs stop whining around the table if we give them some when we are eating.

Sometimes Pa wades along the river bank feeling under the water for holes. When he finds one, he reaches in and often pulls out a big old catfish. We call that kind of fishing "noodling." He has promised to teach me how to do it. I don't know if I want to learn. I hate water snakes. If I reached into a hole and felt a big old snake, I'd just be scared to death. He says I don't have to worry. He has been noodling for years and has never gotten snake-bit. Last year he went to the blacksmith in Evansville, Indiana, and had him make a noodling pole with a hook on the end. Maybe I will learn to noodle with that pole.

The most important wild food for us is deer meat. We eat lots of deer. They make good eating, even if they are pests. They're always trying to get into our fields and garden, so they are easy to hunt. We tan deer hides and use them for all sorts of things such as winter coats and britches. We store extra hides to take to the settlement down-river at Evansville. There we trade for things we need.

Pa goes to town two or three times each year to get things we can't grow or make. He buys gunpowder, lead for bullets, salt by the barrel, coffee, and needles and thread for Ma and Katie. Sometimes he gets a little sugar to make jam. He trades buckskins for these things, and the storekeeper always tells him the price. Salt is ten bucks for a barrel, so Pa knows how many deer hides he has to take to pay for the things he needs.

Pa made the big dugout canoe that we use to trade with along the river. He picked out the biggest, straightest poplar tree on the place and cut it down for the canoe. He shaped the ends with his axe and trimmed off the top side of the log. He built a fire on the top side and began slowly burning away the wood. After it burned a while, he scraped away the charred wood. By burning and scraping, he was able to hollow out the log. It took a long time.

The canoe is big enough to carry the things we need to trade most of the time. We can carry two barrels of salt in it if we're careful. Two people can handle it downstream, but it is hard work to paddle it all the way back up the Green River from Evansville. It takes three or four days for the upstream trip. We camp along the bank. We always take a dog or two to guard the canoe while we sleep.

Salt is the most important thing we have to buy. We use it to preserve our hog meat. We raise a lot of hogs. They feed in the woods and live wild. We earmark them so we will know which ones are ours. We raise the hogs so we can sell the meat. There is always a market for pork.

Fall is hog-killing time. As soon as the weather gets good and cold we kill hogs. We invite folks around us to come and help, and we have a big feast on hog liver and loins. We also grind meat for sausage. Everyone takes home fresh meat for the next day. Hams, bacon, shoulder, and jowls are the best parts of the hog. We cure them with salt and smoke them in the smokehouse over a good hickory fire. When they are cured, they keep for a long time. Then we can sell the cured meat for money to pay our taxes.

The most useful part of the hog is the fat, which is cooked down for lard. We use lard all the time for cooking. Ma also mixes it with lye to make soap. We soak wood ashes in a big hollowed-out log to make lye. We fill up the log with ashes and then pour water into it. After the ashes soak a while and settle to the bottom, we can drain off the lye water. We cook lard in the lye water, cool it, and cut it into bars for soap.

We also use lye water to make one of my favorite foods, hominy. To make hominy we soak shelled corn in lye water for a day or two until the grains swell up and get soft. I like it cooked fresh, but it can also be dried and stored in sacks. Ma grinds the dried hominy into grits and cooks them for breakfast. Grits are really good with a little honey or with the gravy Ma makes with lard and milk.

We work hard in the summer putting up food for the winter. We grow lots of green beans in with our corn. We string the beans on long strings and hang them up under the roof to dry. They are called "leather britches," and they taste pretty good in the winter. We also grow squash and pumpkins in with the corn. We slice them and hang them up to dry the same way.

Ma brought apple seeds with her from Virginia, so we have apple trees. There is nothing better than a hot fried apple pie on a cold winter day. We dry lots of apples and make cider out of the bad ones. Pa sometimes lets the cider get pretty hard. Ma gets mad at him because she doesn't want us kids drinking it.

In July we plant a big patch of turnips to eat in the fall. They will stand in the field until we get really hard frosts. We also grow collards for fall greens. We have a cellar that Pa dug and lined with logs. We put carrots, beets, cabbage, turnips, and potatoes in there and cover them with leaves to protect them from the cold. They won't freeze, and we can eat them all winter long.

In the winter we work hard making things to sell. In a swampy area across the river, we cut cypress trees to use to make shingles. We cut the cypress logs into two-foot sections and split out the shingles. Cypress wood makes good shingles because it does not rot and it ages to a pretty grey color.

We also cut hickory trees and whittle out all kinds of handles. We make handles for hoes, axes, mattocks, hammers, and other tools. Pa makes kegs out of oak, binding the wood together with willow hoops. He uses the kegs to hold the lard that he takes to market.

Our biggest market for trade is in New Orleans. Pa has made three trips to New Orleans. He and Uncle Jim and some other neighbors build flatboats. They float down the Green River to the Ohio, and then to the Mississippi. They load the boats with hams, lard, live hogs, wood handles and shingles, dried apples, barrels of corn—whatever we can spare.

When they get to Louisiana, there is always a market for our goods. Sometimes they sell in the city or at plantations along the river. Sometimes they sell to merchants who ship our goods on big ships to cities in the East. It makes me proud to think that the hams and bacon we raised on our farm might end up in a big city like Philadelphia or Charleston or New York.

Last year Pa heard all about General Andy Jackson and the big battle at New Orleans with the British. I'm glad that war is over and we are free to trade with anybody we want to. It's hard for me to think about trade with other countries, but I know that it's important.

They say that one day tobacco will be really big as a trade item. Pa always grows a little tobacco to make plug for our own use. He says now he is going to grow some to sell down the river, too.

When he was in New Orleans, Pa saw a boat that was run by

steam power. It could move upstream against the current just as easy as pie. It sailed all the way up-river to Louisville.

Pa says it would be a wonder to be able to ride a steamboat back home after floating a flatboat down to New Orleans. Now he has to walk all the way back home along the Natchez Trace. He and Uncle Jim travel with a big group of men so they won't get robbed by the highwaymen who travel along the Trace. It's sad that people can't walk home from New Orleans in safety without fear of being robbed. I don't know what the country is coming to.

In the winter we kids have to study. Ma went to a Dame School back in Virginia. She learned how to read and write and cipher. There are no schools around here, so she teaches us when the weather is too bad to work outside. John and Katie and I can read and write, and we can cipher well enough to get by. We can figure how many acres are in a field, how many board feet of lumber are in a log, and how many bushels of corn are in a corn crib. We also can figure out money so that we won't get cheated in dealing with other people. I don't always like to study, but I know there are lots of things I need to learn. The world is always changing, so I guess I will keep at my studies.

We have a family Bible. We kids take turns reading out loud from it so our parents can see how well we are doing. We talk about what it says. There are no churches around here, but last year we went to a big camp meeting over on the Gasper River. There were more people there than I had ever seen in my life. I heard preaching all day and into the night. People had tents to sleep in, and some folks stayed for two weeks or more.

Lots of people got religion. Ma and Katie got baptized right in the river. I know that Ma would have been happy if Pa and John and I had gotten baptized, too. Pa said it was enough for him to be there while his farm was being neglected. John was too interested in the girls to pay attention to anything else.

I listened to some of the preachers. I guess what they said was true. But it seems to me that if a person is honest with his family and the people he knows and meets, does a full day's work and isn't lazy, and always tells the truth even if it hurts, that's about all anyone can expect.

I noticed that some of the folks who talked most about how God loves everybody were people who owned slaves. That girl that John is so sweet on comes from a family of slave-holders. I don't know how he can deal with that. It just doesn't seem right for one person to be able to own another person, not right at all. At any rate, I sure didn't get converted!

One of the preachers said something good, however. He was talking about Heaven and how beautiful it was. He tried to put it in words we could understand. Finally he said that Heaven was a Kentucky kind of place.

On summer evenings I like to sit on our front step and watch the sun disappear between the beautiful old oak trees. I can look down toward the river and see it shining like gold. I think about what that preacher said. I truly believe that there is no greater place than where I live and no more beautiful sight than sunset on the Green River.

2

Jeff's Family Farm

1849

The family had a big party the other day to mark my 49th birthday. I don't hold much for parties, but I have to admit I had a good time.

We had a lot to celebrate, I guess. Life has been good to me and my family, even with all the ups and downs. It has caused me to take some time to think about all the changes that have taken place over the years. I have a wonderful wife, Elizabeth, and two fine sons, Henry and Joseph. They are both grown now and are a real help on the farm. Elizabeth and I met at a camp meeting. Ma loved camp meetings, and we used to take her when we could. One day I set my eyes on a pretty, slim girl with dark brown curls, and that was that. She was from the upper Green River country, where her folks had a small farm.

Elizabeth and I got married in 1824, so we have been together for a quarter of a century. We are so proud of our two fine boys. We also had two little girls, but they did not live very long. One died just a few days after she was born; the other died when she was two years old. The second summer is hard on little ones, what with starting to eat regular food and all.

They are buried up on the hill behind the barn in our family plot. Ma and Pa are there, and Uncle Jim and Aunt Becky, too.

They have all been dead for some time, but they are all still missed. Uncle Jim and Aunt Becky never did have children. When they died, they left their farm to my sister, Katie, and me. This means that we now have about 400 acres here along the Green River.

Katie still lives here at The Home Place. Her life has not been all that she had hoped for when she was a young girl. She fell in love with a young fellow who came down-river looking for work. We hired him as a farm hand, but we could not pay him very much. He was a proud man. He said he did not want to marry until he had his own place and could provide for a wife.

Katie agreed to wait. He was a hard worker and saved his money. After a few years he set out for Arkansas to get some cheap land. Before he could get settled, he caught a bad fever and died. Katie's heart was just broken when she got the letter from the sheriff in Arkansas telling her about it.

She is 45 years old now and says she has accepted being an old maid. She is a wonderful help to Elizabeth and the children, and we all love her very much. She signed her share of Uncle Jim and Aunt Becky's land over to me, and I promised her she would have a home with us as long as we all live.

I can't believe all the changes that have taken place in the country since I was a young lad. The state of Texas has come into the Union, as well as a lot of other states in the West. We fought a war with Mexico and got a huge amount of land. Now folks have discovered gold way out in California, and people are just crazy to get out there and get rich fast.

I know of some young men from this area that left to go to the gold fields. They don't know any more about mining for gold than I do about sailing a steamboat, but nothing would keep them at home. I guess they figured that pick handles were more exciting than plow handles. I don't see it, but I'm not 20 years old any more either. I'm just glad that our sons Henry and Joseph didn't catch gold fever. They decided to stay here on the farm with us.

I wonder sometimes about my brother John out in Missouri. He married that girl he was so sweet on way back. He had a fine farm there with several slaves that his wife's people brought from Kentucky. The mail service is so bad and our lives are so different that we haven't kept in touch. Maybe some day I will take a steamboat out to Missouri and pay John a visit. That would be something!

I never even saw a steamboat until I was a grown man, and now they are as common as fleas on a dog. In 1828, a steamboat called *The United States* came up the Green and Barren Rivers all the way to Bowling Green. Two years later the Green and Barren River Navigation Company was formed. They began working to get a set of locks and dams built on the rivers. Two years ago, in 1847, the job was done. Now boats can travel with ease between Bowling Green on the Barren River and Evansville, Indiana, on the Ohio River.

The rates are not too high. We can ride the boat from our landing below the house to Evansville for 50 cents. This means that when we float logs to Evansville we can now ride back in style rather than having to paddle for more than 100 miles in a canoe. The modern world is really handy sometimes.

There is even talk of building railroads in Kentucky. People say there are plans to build a line from Louisville to Nashville that would pass right through Bowling Green. Folks talk of a line from Evansville to Nashville as well.

We have gotten into the logging business at The Home Place. Our farm is still mostly timber. The demand for lumber is so great that we can make money cutting logs and floating them down-river to Evansville where there are big sawmills.

Uncle Jim's place south of ours has some bottom land. We cut cypress there, and we get oak, walnut, and wild cherry from the higher ground. We do the cutting in winter when the ground is frozen. It is easier to skid the logs, and the horses don't have to work so hard. It keeps us busy in the winter when there is not as much farm work to do.

We tie the logs together into a big raft and build a little cabin on it. Then we wait for the river to rise and set us on our way. I worried about the dams, but it turns out they are not a problem. When the river is high enough to float our raft, we can go right over the dams with plenty of water to spare. We always hope for a good spring flood so we can have an easy trip to the log market.

Selling logs gives us some cash money, which we need to start the farming season. We buy seeds and supplies in Evansville and carry them back with us.

We also cut up some logs into lumber. We have a saw pit, and when we have some time we saw logs into boards. We roll the logs onto a frame over the pit. The one man gets on top of the log and the other beneath it. We ripsaw out the boards with a big two–man saw. It is hard work, but we take turns working in the pit, where we get covered with sawdust. The saw has to be razor-sharp, so we spend a lot of time with a file sharpening each tooth. We have sawed and cured enough lumber to build a nice house right in front of the old log cabin my pa built. It is a two-story house with a big porch on the west side so we can sit and watch the river and the sunset in the evenings. Katie has a big room upstairs. The boys have moved into the old cabin, so we old folks rattle around in the new house. Ma and Pa would surely be proud of how fine we live now.

We have also built a big tobacco barn. Tobacco has become our most important crop. Now that the steamboats give us a way to get the crop to market easier, we are growing even more. The whole Green River area is becoming a "tobacco patch."

Tobacco is very hard on the soil. We grow our tobacco on the new ground where we have just cut timber. It does well for a few years, but then the soil gets weak. We spread manure from the horse and cow barn onto the tobacco field to help the plants grow. Some of our neighbors make fun of us for doing this, but I believe it makes for a better crop. I got the idea from Ma. She always put manure on the vegetable garden. She was really fussy about her garden. It stills gets a good load of manure every winter. We always have a fine crop from that garden. Ma always said, "We get our living from the fields, but the garden keeps us alive."

There are factories in Louisville that make pipe tobacco, which is very popular these days. Everybody, it seems, smokes a pipe. These factories can't produce enough to meet the demand. We ship tobacco in barrels called hogsheads to Louisville.

We also sell twist, which we make ourselves. We take good tobacco leaves that have been well cured and strip the main stem from the leaf. Then the two half-leaves are flavored with a dip made with honey and whiskey. After the leaves have dried, we wrap them with a broad wrapper leaf and roll them into a tight roll about a foot long. We back-braid the roll, creating a twist of tobacco that fits neatly into a pocket.

People around here like our twist tobacco because it tastes good. You don't have to have a fire to enjoy it like you do with a pipe. You can have a chew of twist and still have your hands free for the plow handles. You can also enjoy it in the barn without running the risk of setting the place on fire.

We also make whiskey. Pa always "ran a little corn," as he put it. Ma didn't like him doing it, but that didn't stop him. It was the easiest way to turn corn into money, he always said. He claimed he learned how to make whiskey from an old Scotsman in Virginia, and he was pretty good at it.

We have a still and make a few barrels every year. Some of it goes for flavoring our tobacco. Some of it we use for medicine to ward off chills in the winter and the "trots" in the summer, you understand. The rest we sell to a saloon-keeper in Evansville who will buy all we can send him.

Most of our corn goes to feed hogs. We raise quite a few hogs. Every year we cure hams, bacons, shoulders and jowls for sale, and we make a lot of lard. There is good money to be made in this business. I intend to use most of my corn for meat in the future and probably will quit making whiskey.

Towns are springing up everywhere around the Green River. A lot more people have moved to the area. They all have to eat, and it's the job of farmers to feed them. We can ship meat and lard by steamboat to markets in Bowling Green, Evansville, Owensboro, Louisville—even Memphis and New Orleans—and all the towns in between.

We still take an occasional flatboat of produce down-river to market. The dams on the Green River have slowed up this trade except during high-water season. The high cost of shipping on steamboats is balanced out by the fact that it makes trade with the cities easier. We can make more money selling our goods in the cities.

The steamboats from Evansville bring us salt for curing our meat. The salt comes from West Virginia and gets delivered to our landing for a charge of 50 cents a ton. We sure can't haul it home for that price. Salt is our biggest expense in the hog business. Now we have a steady supply, thanks to the boats.

We can get just about anything we need from town by trading tobacco or meat. The town merchants all accept what they call "country pay." They will take whatever we have. In the summer we ship potatoes and vegetables, butter, and fruit, whatever we can spare. We buy coffee, sugar, needles and thread, and cloth to make clothes with.

Elizabeth and Katie make most of our clothes from store-bought cloth. The new textile factories back east make all kinds of cloth. We buy shoes and hats in town, but Elizabeth and Katie make everything else. We men don't require fancy clothes, but we always buy a little lace, buttons or other fancy stuff for Elizabeth and Katie when we are in town. My women like that!

Our farm really gives us a fine life. Pa and Ma chose a good spot, all right. It is sometimes hard for me to realize how much things have changed. I look out at a 20-acre field, and I can remember back when it was all just timber. Now we have to plow with a breaking plow and a team of horses. Following a plow all day is hard work, fighting the handles to keep it in the row. I'm glad I have two strong boys to help me out, because I am getting too old for the hardest work these days.

I am also glad we can afford some luxuries to make our lives easier. One day last fall we heard a loud blast coming from the river. Our son Joseph raced down from the field yelling that a steamboat was coming to the landing. A big white boat pulled up. Two strong fellows jumped off and got to work unloading our shiny new cook stove. We moved it into the house, and now Elizabeth and Katie no longer have to cook at the fireplace. The stove burns wood. It has a chamber that keeps water hot, so there is water for washing dishes, shaving, and cleaning up before meals. It even warms the water for our weekly baths. It has an oven, too, so we can have all kinds of baked goods. It's much easier than using the old reflector oven at the fireplace.

We also got a horse-mill to grind grain. We make our own corn meal and wheat flour. Now we can have wheat bread and biscuits. We don't have to live off corn bread all the time. The mill has two stones. The top one is mounted on a shaft, which has a long pole on it. We hitch a horse to the pole. He walks around the mill, turning the upper stone against the lower one. All we have to do is pour in the grain and it is turned to meal or flour.

Without steamboats we could not have things like the kitchen stove or the horse-mill. The cost of transportation would be too high. There still are not any roads to speak of. The counties are supposed to provide roads, but those roads are mostly mudholes. The mud is so deep in wet weather we can't drive on the roads. When it is dry, they are dusty and rough. Besides, few people have wagons that could carry such a load.

We brought the millstones and the stove up from the landing on our ground-sled. We use it to carry heavy things. It has strong wooden runners made out of Osage orange wood. When the ground is just a little wet, it works pretty well, but the horses really have to strain to get it up the hill from the landing. We hauled all the rock for the foundation and chimneys of the new house on the ground-sled.

When I was still a young lad, Pa made our first plow. It was a heavy wooden plow called a bull-tongue. It had a flat wooden blade with an iron plate on it. It broke the ground all right, but it was terrible to use. We had to struggle to keep it in the furrow. Every time it hit a rock or root, it would jerk something awful. Pa was always bruised and sore when he had to plow. That was the plow I learned on. We continued to use it until it wore out, and I built another one like it. But now we have a much better plow. It is factory-made, all iron, with a pointed plowshare that cuts through the dirt and a moldboard that turns over the soil. The plow pulls up the weed and grass roots so they will die. It also breaks up the ground better so it is easier to work. Most important, it has a landside that holds the plow in the furrow so we don't have to fight it all the time.

The new plow lets us work the ground up deeper and cuts through the tangle of the tree roots in new ground. Since we break new ground every few years for tobacco, the plow has eased our work and speeded up the plowing. Plowing is still the hardest job we have to do, but modern equipment has certainly made it easier than it was just a few years ago.

After plowing the field, we "drag" it to break up the clods of dirt. We have two kinds of drags. Both are made out of oak that has been shaped into boards about six inches by twelve inches. The bigger drag uses boards about six feet long that are tied together by cross pieces. We bore holes in the flat side of these boards and pound in hickory pegs so that they form teeth, which break up the dirt. After a few passes over a plowed field with the drag, the clods are broken up, and the field is ready for planting.

If we are planting wheat, we simply throw the seeds by hand over the field. We then drag it to cover the seeds so the birds won't eat them. We plant corn with a hoe. We dig a little hole, drop in three or four corn seeds and a bean or squash or pumpkin seed. Then we cover them up. It takes a lot of time to plant, going back and forth across the field. Little tobacco plants are transplanted by hand from the plant beds to the fields. This is slow work because we have to carry water in buckets to water the plants when we put them into the ground.

To cultivate our crops, we have a cultivator, which is made

much the same way as the drag. It has two long sides which come to a point in front, and a short side in back about two feet wide. It also has hickory teeth. We use this tool to cultivate between rows of young tobacco.

For cultivating corn we use a double-shovel, which is built kind of like a plow. It has two flat blades which are offset so they break up the ground more easily. It digs deeper and throws the dirt toward the corn plant, hilling it up. Of course, we still have to chop the weeds and grass around the plants by hand with hoes. We spend a lot of time in the summer fighting the weeds and grass in our crops and gardens.

About three years ago we got a fine wagon made by a factory in Louisville. It has a heavy frame and wide steel tires on the wheels. It is strong enough to haul big loads, such as tobacco hogsheads, yet we can also ride to meeting in it. How nice it is to travel in comfort, even with the rough roads, rather than having to walk or ride horseback. With the wagon, Elizabeth and Katie are more likely to go somewhere than when they had to walk. Neither of them would ever ride a horse, since we do not have side saddles. They claim that no self-respecting woman would ever ride like a man. We men always ride bareback on the work horses, since we do not have any saddles or saddle horses.

There is a little church not too far from our home. We go there when the weather is pretty. It is a Methodist church served by a traveling preacher who comes by once a month to hold services. The rest of the time a class leader, who is just a local farmer, leads the lesson. In older times, when Elizabeth and I got married, we often had to wait several months for a preacher to come through the area to do services. When people died, we just had to bury them. Later, when a preacher came by, we would hold a funeral service.

Elizabeth likes the church because it gives her a chance to be with other women. I know that she gets really lonely on the farm, not seeing anybody but family for days on end. Katie, on the other hand, takes great comfort from the church. She has always been religious, ever since she got religion as a young girl. Now, with the death of her man, she has become even more so. It is a good thing that she finds that comfort.

I wish I could find comfort in what is going on in our nation. I have a great fear that we are headed toward awful times. The question of slavery and the spread of slavery into the new lands in the West has people really worked up. It seems that the arguments are getting hotter. Both sides seem to believe that they are morally right and that God is on their side. I fear for what the future might bring if this question can't be settled. I fear for my sons, who will have to deal with whatever the future holds and whatever decisions the government makes.

3

Henry Keeps the Tradition

1880

We buried Daddy a few weeks ago. He lived a long life—80 years. Afterwards we were going through his things and found the stories he had written about his boyhood and his life on the farm. I was so impressed that I decided, for the sake of the children, to add my story as well.

It's now 1880. When Daddy was born here, the year after his parents came from Virginia, the Green River country was a wilderness. In his old age he could ride in comfort to Louisville on a passenger train. He was a good man who loved life, loved his farm, and loved his family. I'm just sad that the last 15 years of his life had to be without poor Momma.

She died in 1865, the year the Civil War ended. She was as much a victim of that war as any soldier who died on the battlefield. She died of grief, I believe, over the loss of my brother, Joseph, who died the year before in Virginia. They sent his body home, and he was buried up on the hill. Momma soon joined him. Now Daddy's there, too.

All of our loved ones who have died are in the burying ground except Aunt Katie. She signed her rights to the farm over to Daddy in 1858 and moved to South Union, Kentucky. She joined a religious group there called the Shakers. I recall she was always very religious. She lived there until she died in 1878. She is buried in their cemetery at South Union, which is on the railroad from Bowling Green to Memphis.

I guess I should start out talking about the war. In 1861 at the start of the war I joined up with a Kentucky regiment on the Southern side. I got elected lieutenant, since I was a lot older than most of the boys. We were part of the Confederate Army in Tennessee. I believed that the South was right. I held no stock in slavery—never believed in it at all. I did believe that the U.S. government had no right to tell people in the states what they should or should not do. The states should be free to decide things for themselves.

My brother, Joseph, traveled up to Ohio and joined a Union regiment just a few weeks after I left. He really believed that the war was about slavery, which he hated. We both thought we were fighting for freedom—him for freedom for the slaves, me for freedom for the states. It just broke our parents' hearts to have us fighting on opposite sides. Thank Heaven Joseph was sent to Virginia to fight rather than where I was fighting.

We "Johnny Rebs" fought in a few little battles. Then in early 1862 we found ourselves at Fort Donelson, Tennessee, on the Cumberland River, just south of the Kentucky line. The Yanks attacked us with a huge army. They were too strong for us, and we had to give up. I got shot in the right arm. The bullet broke the bone right above my elbow. The doctors had to cut my arm off below the shoulder.

I was in the hospital when we surrendered, but was too weak to be marched to a prison camp. They put me on a hospital boat with other wounded men and sent me to a hospital in Evansville, Indiana. It was a big place called The Marine Hospital, and it was full of the wounded. I got better in a few weeks. I gave my word that I would never fight again, and they let me go home. I took a steamboat home from Evansville and got dropped off at our own landing.

Daddy cried when he saw me coming slowly up the hill. I had never seen my Daddy cry before. That was worse than being wounded. I think my coming home made it harder for my parents in a way. Seeing me without my arm made them fear even more the dangers Joseph faced every time he went into battle. It is easier for people to accept war when they don't see the reality of it every day.

Joseph fought for two years in Virginia and never got more than a scratch. Then in 1864 he caught some sort of fever and died, just like that. I was in the army for ten months and thought I was unlucky to lose an arm. Poor Joseph had to go through all that hell for two and a half years. Then he died of some sickness. Life just doesn't make sense sometimes.

We were lucky here on the farm. The war mostly bypassed us. The Rebels wanted to blow up the locks on the Green River at Rochester. General Buckner, who was a Kentuckian, ordered the locks to be jammed with logs instead. The Yanks finally got all of the logs pulled out. They were able to use the river to supply their forces in southern Kentucky. We saw their boats pass by our landing, but they didn't bother us. We guessed it was because Joseph was in their army.

The Rebel forces didn't bother us either. Our farm was not

easy to get to by road, and they didn't have any boats. Maybe it was because of me, since everybody around here knew of my service in the Confederate Army.

At any rate we were able to keep the farm going during the war. Daddy had to work extra hard. As I got stronger, I did all I could, but farming is a pretty hard job for a one-armed man. My own boys really worked hard. They did the work of grown men, even though they were still only children.

I have not told about my family. I married my wife, Mary, in 1853, long before the war. We had three children: Little Jeff was born in 1855; John was born in 1857; and our daughter, Selena, came along in 1861. Poor Mary had a really hard time with Selena, and the baby girl died in a few days. Mary was sick for a long time, and she was never able to have more children.

Our family does not seem to have much luck raising girls, but we sure have been lucky with our two boys. I don't know what Mary and Daddy and I would have done without them. They were able to do just about everything that we needed. When they were still small, they could harness and drive the horses, care for the animals, and help take goods to market. About the only job they could not do during the war years was plowing, so Daddy had to do all that, even though he was really too old. We cut down on the amount of ground we broke until the boys got old enough to plow. I'm sorry the boys had to work so hard when they were so young, but I'm thankful they were not old enough to go to war.

Momma sure was proud of her grandsons, and they were her only source of happiness in her last few months. She felt her life

A breaking plow in an ad from 1890.

was over after the death of Joseph. But the world goes on. It seems hard to believe, but the 15 years since the end of the war have been very good for us. Tobacco has brought us good times, and we have been able to add a lot to the farm.

The soil in the Green River Valley is good for raising tobacco. We have to keep clearing new ground for a high grade-crop, and we also use manure. Daddy was a great believer in fertilizing with manure. I hated the job of spreading it, but it makes a much higher grade of tobacco. Since we get more money for higher grades, it is worth the effort.

The tobacco we grow is called Pryor. It's a rich, smooth leaf used for making pipe tobacco mostly, and for twist. Some of it gets sent to Canada, where they make it into plug chewing tobacco. Pryor does best in the rich soil of new land where there is good drainage and a lot of loam from rotted leaves. Rich soil gives the leaf a light body and a good texture. The leaf cures into a bright brown color, which grades high.

Pryor is also a good stemming tobacco. We used to sell our tobacco ourselves, but since the war, a whole new way of marketing tobacco developed. Owensboro is the center of our tobacco market. There are 18 tobacco factories there, called stemmeries. We sell our tobacco to their agents, who come to our barn. They buy the tobacco and arrange to have it shipped to Owensboro.

In the stemmeries they strip the large center stem from each leaf, which makes two half-leaf strips. The strips age for several weeks in big wooden barrels, called hogsheads, which hold about 1,200 pounds each. Most of the strips are sold to England, but some go to the "Regie." That is our name for the state tobacco companies in the other European countries. Smoking is very popular in Europe, and American tobacco is the best.

The buyers for these stemmeries travel around visiting our farms after we have cut and stripped our tobacco. After it is cured in the barn, and when the humidity is right for the leaf to come "in order" and get soft as good leather, we strip the leaves from the main stalk. We sort the leaves into three grades: trash, lugs, and leaf.

After the leaves are sorted, we tie them into bundles called hands. Five or six leaves are bundled together with the stems even. The head of the bundle is wrapped with a leaf folded into a strip about an inch wide. This tie–leaf is secured by tucking the stem end through the center of the bundle.

The price we get depends on the grade of the leaf. Last year, in 1879, we got from 50 cents to $1 per hundred pounds for trash; $2 to $4 per hundred for lugs; and $4 to $8 per hundred for leaf. You can see why we work hard to produce the highest grade we can. It really pays when we have a high-grade leaf.

We still make some twist tobacco for our own use and to sell to our old customers. Several big companies make twist tobacco now. They sell it at such a low price that we can't compete with them and still make any money. Besides, we are getting too busy to fool with it, except for our own use. Now that we have quit making whiskey, we have to buy it by the jug for flavoring. I think we will quit making twist completely now that Daddy is gone. He was an expert roller and really seemed to get a lot of fun out of making twist. For me it was just another job. A one-armed man is no good as a tobacco roller. My boys don't like it, either. They are pipe smokers.

We have been playing around with a new kind of tobacco called burley or white burley. It is a strong plant and produces a beautiful leaf. It started in Virginia as red burley, but some farmers in Ohio got a light-colored leaf from their seeds, so they call it white burley. It is getting to be popular as a blending leaf in pipe tobaccos, especially with people who roll the tobacco into cigarettes. Cigarette smoking is catching on in some places, but I don't think it will ever be popular. Folks around here will stick with twist or plug or pipes.

We are doing well enough on The Home Place that we have

been able to get some fancy new equipment for the farm. In 1870, we bought a sulky plow. It is like a walking plow, only it's mounted on wheels so we can ride. Since we don't have to guide it with handles, I can even plow with the riding plow. It took me quite a while to learn how, and my furrows were pretty ragged for a while, but I eventually got the hang of it. When we come to the end of a furrow, we just pull on a lever and the plow lifts out of the ground. It really speeds up the plowing, and we don't have to drag the plow by hand to turn it around for the next furrow. I'm glad that I can now do my share of this job, although I sometimes have to guide the team with the reins between my teeth to free my one hand to work the lever.

We also bought a riding cultivator for corn. It saves us a lot of time in keeping the weeds out of the corn crop. It took me quite a while to learn to use it with just one arm, but now I handle it easily. We also bought a grain drill, which speeds the planting of all sorts of small grains such as wheat, oats, rye and barley.

We are growing a lot of wheat these days, and we have just bought a binder. This machine cuts the grain and ties it into sheaves. We stack the sheaves into shocks in the field so that the grain will dry completely. When the threshing machine arrives, we go out in wagons, load up the sheaves of grain, and bring them in to be threshed.

Threshing time is quite a circus. The threshing machine is a wonder! It is powered by a big steam traction engine. It has a big power take-off wheel that is connected to the threshing machine by a big leather belt. We feed the sheaves of grain into the thresher, and grain comes out. It is bagged up into gunny sacks

A sulky plow in an ad from 1890.

or loaded into wagons. We sack up the grain that we are going to sell so we can ship it on board the steamboats to market. The grain we are going to feed our animals, such as oats, we load into wagons to take to the barn.

The straw gets blown out of another part of the machine. Every year our straw stack gets bigger as we grow more grain. They say the bigger the straw stack, the better the farm. If that's so, our farm is pretty good. We use the straw for bedding for our animals and put it around our strawberries and other small fruit to protect them during the winter. We also pack vegetables in straw to keep in the root cellar.

Gangs of people get together to work at threshing time. Neighbors help each other. It's a party as well as hard work. The women help out in the kitchen and get to talk with each other. There is always a world of food. We have fried chicken, fresh vegetables, lots of bread, and all sorts of fruit pies and cakes. Hard work sure makes people hungry! That old cook stove doesn't get much chance to cool off during threshing time.

There is a good market for wheat these days. Most towns have a flour mill. We ship our wheat to a big mill in Evansville. We use the oats to feed the horses on the farm. Our rye gets sold to a distillery in Owensboro. Our barley goes to a brewery in Evansville. We send corn, when we have plenty, to the distilleries in Owensboro.

We still ship our hogs to market by boat. We no longer kill hogs at home, except for our own use. The packing plants in Evansville and Owensboro are always a good market for hogs. We have even shipped them as far as Louisville. It is quite a job to get a big old lard hog, which might weigh up to 1,000 pounds, to walk up the chute onto the deck of a steamboat! The passengers are not happy when they see us with a big lot of hogs to load. It means a smelly trip for them.

A lot of railroads have been built in Kentucky in the last few years, but the steamboats are still best for us. The first railroad in this area was the Louisville & Nashville, which passed through Bowling Green. The next was the Elizabethtown & Paducah, which crossed the Green River at Rockport in Ohio County. In the past few years a line called the Owensboro & Russellville crossed the Green at Livermore. We can send goods by boat to Livermore, and then by train to Owensboro, but it is expensive. It is still cheaper for us to use the boats to Evansville.

Besides, the boats are good customers of ours. We sell lots of butter, milk, eggs, and fresh garden produce to the boats for use in their kitchens. We used to cut fire wood for the boats as well. They wanted it cut four feet long in stacks four feet high and 84 feet long. It was a lot of work. While we had a lot of timber in the bottoms, we could make money doing it. Now most of our timber near the river is gone.

We still cut logs. We sell white oak to the barrel-makers in Owensboro for whiskey barrels. Bourbon whiskey has to be aged in virgin white oak barrels. We call white oaks "whiskey trees" because that is mostly what they are used for these days. We also cut a lot of walnut and cherry and sell them to the furniture plants in Tell City, Indiana.

We have new things for the house, too. We got some nice furniture at the plant that buys our walnut lumber. I got Mary a sewing machine. She is proud of it and is quite good on it. It took her a while to learn how to work the treadle just right to make it sew like she wanted.

We have new Mason jars for canning. Mary puts up fruits and vegetables in the summer, and we eat them all winter long. She keeps the cellar full of jams and jellies, and jars of corn, beans, English peas and other garden truck. When we butcher hogs, we make sausage that she cans as well. It is a hard, hot job, but the boys help her as best they can. It's too bad baby Selena died. She would have been a big help to her Momma.

We buy canned goods at the store sometimes. The variety of food that city people have is amazing. The stores in towns have oranges and bananas all the time and fresh meat whenever we want it. They also have candy, cheeses, crackers, and all sorts of good things. But they are expensive. In Owensboro, country hams and lard sell for 10 cents a pound and bacon for 11 cents. Butter is 20 cents a pound and eggs 10 cents a dozen. I don't see how city folks can afford to eat!

We have more social life here on the farm than my parents ever had. We now have a school down at the crossroads. The teacher boards around with the families of some of her pupils. The school offers eight grades, which is probably enough. There is a college in Bowling Green where students can go if they want more, but it costs a lot. Our church has a new building and many more members. We now have a preacher two Sundays a month and lessons every Sunday. There are socials, dinners on the grounds, and revivals in the summer.

We have a baseball team. Little Jeff and John both play, and they get up games with other teams up and down the river. It is quite an event, and everyone turns out to watch the baseball boys.

Roads are our biggest problem. The roads now are not much better than in my daddy's day. I got so mad when my wagon got stuck a few years ago that I ran for the office of magistrate. Much to my surprise, I got elected! I have been working hard to get the landowners to bring the roads into better shape. They need to be ditched, crowned, and graded to keep them smooth. We also need better bridges. I got re-elected last year, so it seems that a lot of people agree with me. Some day we will have all-weather roads, maybe even with rock.

I started out this account talking about death. I'll end it by talking about life and hope for the future. Little Jeff is getting married next week when the preacher comes through. He is marrying Jean Durham, the daughter of neighbors—fine folks who go to our church. Mary has been bustling around for weeks making him a fine suit and shirt and other clothes for his new life. There is just no telling what kind of confusion is going on over at the Durhams'.

Little Jeff and Jean are going to live here with us at The Home Place. We have plenty of room, and Mary will sure enjoy having another woman around. John will be moving out soon. He plans to marry a lovely girl from Simpson County whose parents have a little dairy farm. She is an only child, and John loves working with cows, so he will be all set. John and his bride-to-be met at a baseball game, of all things!

I only hope that Jeff will be content to stay on the farm and raise his family here. So many young people today are attracted to the cities and the big jobs in factories. It would just break my heart if my boys abandoned the land for the city, but I would never tell them. My dream is that one day my grandchildren will live here on the farm my grandfather hacked out of the wilderness. Only time will tell, I reckon.

4

The Tractor

1952

My name is Joe Bob Boyd. It is really Joseph Robert, but everybody calls me Joe Bob. I am the son of Little Jeff Boyd and the grandson of Henry Boyd. I am the fifth generation of Boyds to farm this land we all call The Home Place.

My family has been after me to write down my story like those who came before me. I am not much for writing, but my daughter Sarah has promised to help, and she's a teacher. So here goes.

I was born in 1901, at the start of the 20th century. That's just about 100 years after my great-grandfather, Thomas Jefferson Boyd, was born here after his parents moved from Virginia. I have seen more changes than any of my ancestors could have dreamed of in a million years. Our farm has been transformed in my lifetime by machines and new inventions. Farming has changed beyond belief, yet it still stays the same. We still depend on the forces of nature for survival, but now we help nature out with fertilizer and better ways of farming.

The Home Place was a fine farm when I was growing up. We had lots of crop land and three work teams of horses. My daddy was very good with horses. He was able to train the teams so they knew just what to do. We could drive them sometimes just by using our voices.

I do love horses. I learned to drive long before I was big enough to harness a team. I was able to do most of the jobs around the place by the time I was ten years old. I had seen the steam engines that ran the threshing machine, of course, and heard tell of tractors being sold to work on farms. Some folks were even predicting that one day farmers would have automobiles to go to town and tractors to farm the land, but I did not believe it.

When I was 16 I lied about my age and joined the army. America had entered the World War, and I wanted to go to France and do my bit for my country. It about broke my mother's heart, but she let me go. The army used horses, and I thought I could work with them. Instead the army sent me to school to be a mechanic. I learned all about gasoline engines. I spent my time in France in a big repair shop working on military trucks and tractors. I realized then that these things were the way of the future. I was lucky to get in on the ground floor with my army training.

At the end of the war, as I was waiting to be shipped home from France, I got a telegram. It said that my daddy and grandad were both dead. The flu was spreading all over the world. Dad and Grandad both got it and died. They had been working so hard to keep the farm going that they were worn out and could not fight the disease. Many soldiers were sick, but somehow I stayed healthy. They say that the flu of 1918 killed more people than the whole war!

The army shipped me home right away. I had to take over running the farm, and I was not yet 18 years old. We had one hired man. As men came home from the army, we were able to get some more help. Still we barely kept the farm going. Good workers were hard to find because they could get better jobs in the cities. I knew that we could not hire the kind of people we wanted. We needed to get more work with less manpower.

The tractor solved this problem. We bought a Fordson tractor in 1920 from a dealer in Owensboro and shipped it by steamboat to our landing. It was a proud day when we unloaded it, and I drove it up the lane from the landing. It had rained during the night and the lane was slick with mud. The big lugs on the steel wheels of the tractor dug right in, and it did not slip a bit coming up the hill. It had a power take-off so we could use it to run other machines, such as a feed mill or little saw mill if we wanted. I worked in France with Fordsons and knew them to be good machines. I knew, too, that I could keep it running. If it broke down I would be able to fix it.

We had a big barbecue to celebrate the arrival of the tractor. Momma and I invited the neighbors and all the folks from our church to see it. A lot of the older men were doubtful. They said we would go broke trying to keep it running. Many of the younger men, however, were eager to ask me all kinds of questions. I could tell that they were thinking that some day they might get a tractor, too.

The barbecue was fun, but there were also some surprises.

A 1920 Fordson tractor.

Our neighbors, the Bishops, were there, and they brought their daughter Betty. When I left for the army, she was a little freckle-faced girl with her bright red hair in pigtails. Now she was a beautiful young lady of 16. I was sure glad we had that barbecue!

The tractor was the star of the show that day. I was proud that ours was the first farm in the neighborhood to own one. I was so eager to put it to work. That night, after our company had left, I spent a lot of time thinking about Dad and Grandad. What would they have said about us being so modern? Finally I decided that they would have liked it, and I went right to sleep.

The tractor did an even better job than I had hoped. We

began to rely on it more and more. I sold two of the horse teams, keeping only two mares and a horse to breed. I enjoyed raising and training horses. I guess I really didn't want to think that the farm would change so much that horses would not still be needed.

We still used horses for lots of jobs during this time. We used them to break the garden and plant beds and to cultivate the garden and tobacco. We also used teams in wet weather to haul things with the wagon. The tractor tended to pack the soil down when it was damp, which was bad for the garden and plant beds. It made ruts in wet weather that tended to wash, causing little ditches. The horses still had a role to play, and I was glad of that.

The tractor changed our crop production, too. We did not have to grow as much oats, since we were feeding fewer horses. On the other hand, we had to raise more crops such as tobacco to sell for cash. We had expenses with the tractor that we did not have with horses. We had to have money coming in to pay the tractor payments and to buy gasoline and spare parts. I began to learn the problems of paying bills and keeping enough cash on hand.

We still shipped most of our products by river. I joined a group called the Good Roads Club to get the county court to improve the roads in our area. It was the same fight my grandad fought years before. We wanted gravel, all-weather roads so we could get our goods to town and get good mail service.

The post office began rural free delivery of mail right before I was born. But the roads were in such bad shape that the mail could not always get through. We needed roads fit to drive on, which meant a gravel surface and good drainage.

I got our first truck in 1923. It was a Model T Ford pickup. That truck really changed our lives. It was a wedding present for my wife, Betty, and me. We were married shortly after I got the truck. We drove all the way to Owensboro to spend the weekend for a honeymoon. I had been courting Betty ever since the night of the big barbecue to celebrate the tractor. She was 19 when we married, and I was 22 years old.

We have really been blessed in our married life. We have had three wonderful children: Frank was born in 1925; Billy in 1927; and Sarah in 1929. Our life has been so much easier than my parents' life. Things we take for granted would have been luxuries for them. We have store-bought bread all the time and fresh meat all year round. We get newspapers and magazines by mail. We are able to talk to people by telephone whenever we want.

We also have a radio. Our first radio was a crystal set that I got in town one day and put together. It ran off a battery that was charged by a charger hooked up to the windmill. We could get a Louisville station and a Nashville station most of the time. It was really a miracle to be able to hear music being played in Louisville or Nashville while we stayed right in our kitchen. Now we have a newer radio.

Yet some things are still the same. We still put up most of our food. We have our garden and orchard, and Momma and Betty can hundreds of quarts of fruits and vegetables every year. We still butcher hogs for our own use and cure our own hams and bacon. You just can't beat a good ham that has been properly cured and aged. Some homemade things are just better than store-bought.

When the children were young, I wanted to get a telephone. Some of us got together and paid to get the poles and wires so we could get phone service. It was a happy day when we got our telephone. The phone hung on the wall in the living room. It had a crank on the side to call the operator. We had an eight-party line. All of us were on the same line, but we each had our own ring, so we would know who the call was for. Our ring was two longs, a short, and a long, like a locomotive whistling for a crossing.

We have better schools now. Our school is still a one-room building, but we have a teacher who has taken some classes at the Teachers College in Bowling Green. Every summer she goes back to take more classes. Soon she will leave us for a better-paying job in a school in town, but the kids are gaining from her knowledge while she is here.

The school is a real center for our community. We still have our baseball team, and the women have all sorts of activities that take place at the school house. They get together for quilting and gossip every month. They also have a home economics teacher who teaches new ways of doing things around the house, cooking, and such. She gives out some good recipes, and once in a while the men are invited for a cakewalk or some other festivity.

We like to go to the high school to watch the basketball games. Every little town has a high school now, and there are bitter rivalries in sports. I never got a chance to go beyond the eighth grade, but I hope my kids can go to high school. They can learn a lot of practical things. The government has a program to provide classes in vocational agriculture and home economics, so boys and girls can learn things they can use in their daily lives. They can also learn bookkeeping, which you need to know if you are going to be a successful farmer these days.

Our church is the real cornerstone of our little community. We can go every Sunday now that we have our truck and the roads are graded more often. The county has finally bought motorized graders to keep the roads in better shape. The motorized graders are a lot faster than the old graders that were pulled by mule teams. They have also begun putting rock on the roads. It's about time, I say!

We finally got the pickup paid for. We were completely out of debt by the time our daughter, Sarah, was born in 1929. I began to think about getting a more powerful tractor and a new truck. Every time I would get my mind made up to do it, a little voice inside me said to wait, so I waited.

Thank Heavens I did, because late in 1929 the stock market crashed. The economy of the whole country began to fall apart. We entered what came to be called the Great Depression. Prices for farm crops fell to just about nothing. People who had borrowed money or had mortgages on their farms were in real trouble. Before long, banks began to foreclose on mortgages and loans. A lot of people lost their farms and homes.

I was glad I had listened to that little voice. I could keep the old Fordson and the Model T running a lot cheaper than I could pay off loans on new ones. We cut down on expenses and were able to get by. We made fewer trips to town and ate what we grew. Betty made a lot of our clothes, and little Sarah wore a lot of feed-sack dresses growing up, but we survived and kept our farm.

Some of our neighbors lost their land and became tenants on the land they once had owned. Others made room for relatives who moved back home from the cities after they lost their jobs in factories that shut down. Everybody just did what they had to do to help one another.

The steamboats on the Green River were a casualty of the depression. The last of the Green River boats burned in 1930 and was not replaced. There was not enough business to support even one little boat. Most goods went by truck or train, and the boats just could not survive. It was truly the end of an era.

The main highways were paved between Owensboro and Bowling Green and between Elizabethtown and Paducah. Road improvements continued even during the depression. At last we were able to get out of the mud for sure. Good roads made it a lot easier to ship products by truck. We could get baby chicks by express from hatcheries, so we expanded our chicken production. We built a new henhouse and began selling lots of eggs. The better roads made it possible to get to the market in town twice a week with eggs, which brought in much-needed cash.

Franklin D. Roosevelt got elected president in 1932. He promised a "New Deal" for the American people. Soon a great number of government programs started up. The U.S. government gave farm loans so people would not lose their land. Farm prices leveled out and even began to go up a little. Finally we could make a little profit. New government plants provided cheap chemical fertilizers to improve crop yields. Times began to perk up a bit, and we were able to save some money.

I took a big gamble in 1936. I bought a new tractor, a big green John Deere. I also bought a used 1934 Chevrolet sedan. Betty needed the car because the kids were getting bigger and needed to be taken to school and to other activities. I kept the old Fordson, but the new John Deere took over the heavy work on the farm. It was more powerful and easier to drive.

Our older son, Frank, learned to drive the tractor right away. He was 11 years old and a natural mechanic. He loved anything with a motor in it and took to the tractor right away. Soon he could plow a furrow as straight as any grown man. When Billy got to be 11, I taught him to drive, too. Of course, Sarah demanded to learn as well, so when she got old enough I taught her. Soon she could do as good a job as any man. My mother knew how to drive a team, and my wife could drive a car, so I couldn't think of any reason why my daughter should not drive a tractor. When World War II came along, we were all glad she could!

We listened to the news on the radio. When the war broke out in Europe, we all prayed that America could keep out of it. We had enough problems at home, we thought. The war did help the farmers because the demand for all kinds of farm products increased. Prices rose, and we began to make more money.

We heard about the attack on Pearl Harbor after we got home from church on Sunday, December 7, 1941. The next day we forgot all about stripping tobacco. We sat around the radio to listen to President Roosevelt ask Congress for a declaration of war. Betty and I were worried sick about our kids. Frank was 16—the same age I was when I went off to World War I.

As soon as he turned 17, Frank joined the Marine Corps. I signed the papers so he could join, even though I would rather have cut off my hand off. I knew what pain my parents went through back in 1917. Frank went off for training and then came home on leave before being shipped overseas. We never saw him again. He got killed in the South Pacific on some little island that is not even on most maps. We hung a little flag with a gold star on it in the front window in his honor. We were proud of him for being a brave soldier and doing his duty, but all of our pride and his bravery would never bring him back.

Billy and Sarah did the work of grown men on the farm during the war. Billy was drafted out of high school in 1945, right at the end of the war. Thank Heaven the war ended before he was sent into combat. He was sent overseas to Germany as part of the occupation forces.

Sarah stayed in school, and in 1947 she became the first member of our family to graduate from high school. She won a scholarship to Western Kentucky State Teachers College. We drove her to Bowling Green to register. She studied home economics and graduated in 1951. She got a job teaching at our high school and moved back home so she could help out on the farm.

Billy stayed in the army until 1947. He married a girl from Cleveland, Ohio, whom he met while he was in the service. They came back to the farm after he was discharged. His wife, Sally, was a city girl, and she was not happy on the farm. After

Sarah graduated, Billy and Sally moved to the Cleveland area. They bought a little home in Parma, a suburb of Cleveland. Billy got a job in a big Ford Motor Company plant not far away.

So with Frank dead and Billy in Cleveland, it is now up to Sarah to keep The Home Place going. She is engaged to a fine young man named Richard Wines, her high school sweetheart. Richard went to the University of Kentucky, where he studied agriculture.

They plan to marry in the summer of 1953 and live here. Sarah will keep her teaching job and Richard will operate the farm. Another generation of Boyds will keep The Home Place going. All the Boyds in the family burying ground up on the hill must be smiling at that thought!

5

Sarah's Story

1994

It's a tradition, now, to write in this old book started by my great-great grandfather. I'm the first woman to write in it. The farm is mine now.

I want to start my part of our family's story by telling about the best day and the worst day of my life. The best day was my wedding to Richard Wines in 1953. It was held in the front yard of The Home Place, under the shade of the grove of oak trees. With the warm sun coming through the leaves, it was a perfect spot for a wedding.

That same day, Richard and I drove to Nashville for our honeymoon. We stayed at the Maxwell House, a fancy hotel downtown. We saw the Grand Old Opry and shopped at the big department stores. Nashville, the state capital of Tennessee, has a beautiful capitol building at the top of a hill. We even drove out to see President Andrew Jackson's home.

When we came back to Kentucky we moved into the old house with Mom and Dad. It would have been nice to have our own place, but they insisted. We all got along pretty well. The farm was close to the school where I was teaching and to Richard's job at the grain company. It was a good thing we both had jobs, as it turned out.

The worst day of my life was in February of 1955. I was pregnant with little Henry, our first child. I woke up in the middle of the night and smelled smoke. I woke Richard, and he woke Mom and Dad. Somehow we got downstairs and out the front door. There was nothing we could do but watch as the flames roared and old house burned to the ground. We lost everything we had except for the stories my forefathers had written. They were safe in a bank box in town. Everything else went up in smoke.

It was a good thing that we had insurance. The fire started in a broken flue when the chimney got too hot. When we got our settlement from the insurance company, we decided to rebuild. We built two smaller houses rather than one big one. One was a small, two-bedroom house for Mom and Dad. Ours was a bigger house with three bedrooms, since we had a baby on the way. Both houses were the new ranch style with modern furnaces and good wiring. Now farm people live as comfortably as people in town.

After the fire, Richard and I did talk about moving to town. We decided we wanted to stay here and let our baby have the same kind of childhood we had. Growing up on the farm is a special thing, and we wanted that life for our kids. In 1957, two years after little Henry was born, we had our daughter, Debbie. Our family was complete.

Of course they did not have the same kind of childhood I had. Time does not stand still. The one-room school was gone by the time they were old enough to attend. Now we have a new consolidated school. It has separate grades and lots of things to help kids learn, such as colorful maps and a good library. The teachers all have college training, too.

Transportation is no problem. The kids ride new yellow buses to school. We live on one of the school bus routes. The county school district has a whole fleet of buses to carry kids to school. The only problem is the weather. When it snows or floods, they cancel school because the buses can't get through. When I was a girl we went to school no matter what the weather because it was nearby and we could walk.

When our children got old enough to start elementary school, I went back to my job teaching home economics at the high school. Richard wanted me to stay home, but I told him my job was important to me. I studied hard to become a teacher, and I was proud of my career. I love teaching, and my income really helped when we had to buy new equipment for the farm or things for the house. I put aside a part of my salary each month for our children's education.

Going back to work meant that I really had a lot to do at home in the evening. One thing never changes on the farm, and that is the work! We don't have the same chores as our parents and grandparents, but we still have lots of them. We got rid of all the horses, the hens, and the milk cows. Now we don't have to be home to milk every morning and night. We just keep beef cattle and hogs. They don't need the daily care that chickens and milk cows did. We can even go away for a weekend now and then, as long as someone will help feed the animals.

I grew up having to work with the chickens. I gathered the eggs, washed them, boxed them in paper cartons, and got them ready for market. I helped my dad with the milking and had to clean up the equipment each day. I don't miss any of that! I'm happy to get my milk and eggs from the store.

When I was in high school we finally got rid of the old wood cooking range and got a new stove. We also got a furnace. Both the new stove and the furnace burned propane. We put in a big propane tank behind the house. A truck from town comes out to fill it up when we needed more gas. We no longer have to chop the wood and carry it inside for the stove or carry out the ashes. Without all that mess, the house is a lot cleaner. People who talk about the "good old days" have forgotten how hard we worked just to cook our food and keep the house warm and clean. Give me the "good modern days" every time!

Also, when I was in high school, we got electricity. The REA (rural electric agency) brought their lines through in 1947. We finally got electric lights and a refrigerator. A few years later we got a big freezer. How much easier it is to freeze fruits and vegetables than having to can them in jars! We do still can a few vegetables. I think green beans are better canned, but I love that freezer!

The Korean War began in 1950 when I was in college. Richard was drafted, but he did not have to go to Korea, thank goodness. Our neighbor Bob Cline was killed in that war. He and I were good friends. We had gone to school together since first grade.

We got a TV set in 1956. Daddy and Richard said they wanted to watch the political convention, but I think they really wanted to watch the World Series and the football games. It was a black-and-white set with a ten-inch screen. We got a great big antenna, but the picture was often fuzzy because we were so far away from the stations. Of course, now we have a big color TV and a satellite dish, so we get more channels than anyone can watch.

Having electricity meant we could also have a good water system. We put in an electric pump and a big pressure tank that serves both houses. We built two bathrooms in each of the houses and a laundry room as well. We put in a big water heater, and now we have all the hot water we want. I remember as a girl taking my bath in a tin tub in the middle of the kitchen on Saturday night. Those were not "good old days" by any means.

So many changes have happened in our family. Dad passed away in 1972 and Mom died in 1977. Uncle Billy retired in 1978 from his job in Cleveland and wanted to come back with Aunt Sally to The Home Place. Since Mom and Dad's house was empty, they moved in there. We were glad to have them with us. Billy always came home every year to help us strip tobacco. It was good to have his help here. But they both died, too, in the 1980s.

Our children, Henry and Debbie, are grown up now. Henry went to the University of Kentucky like his father and got his degree in agriculture. We were thankful that Henry did not have to go into the army. The war in Vietnam was still going on when he turned 18, but he got a high number in the draft lottery, so he did not have to serve. Several boys from our area did go to Vietnam, however, and two were killed. I had taught both of them in high school. What a waste!

We thought Henry might never marry since he was nearly 40 years old and still single. Then he met a lovely woman, Marjorie, at a Farm Bureau convention. Turned out she was the widow of one of his college friends. Her husband had been killed in a car wreck. Henry and Marjorie got married about a year ago at our church. They moved into Mom and Dad's house, which has been empty since Uncle Billy and Aunt Sally died.

Our Debbie went to Western Kentucky University, where I went many years ago. She loved science and went on to medical school at the University of Louisville. She is now a doctor and lives in California. It is hard for me to realize that my little girl is a doctor and is living so far away from The Home Place. She seems happy out there, and that is what is most important. She comes back to visit now and then. We try to get out to San Francisco in January when the farm work eases up. Now that I am retired from teaching, I go out there by myself sometimes just to see her.

Richard and Henry have worked hard so our farm can make a profit. Farming today is so different from the way it was even in the 1950s. We have decided to spend our time growing grain and raising cattle and hogs. That way we get the best use of our equipment and land.

My dad just kept a hog lot with a few head of hogs, but times have really changed the hog business. We now have a large hog house. We breed our sows to our own boars, and we can decide just when the pigs will be born.

Kentucky has some really big hog operations now, but we

don't want to get any bigger. I hope we can stay in the hog business, but it is hard to compete against the really big farms.

Handling animal waste carefully is important on our farm. All the waste goes into a pond where it ferments. Then we pump it out and spread it on the fields as fertilizer and plow it under. That way there is not much odor. Since our hog pens are not close to any neighbors, the smell does not bother anyone. We do not cause any pollution of the water system.

We finally stopped growing tobacco ourselves and leased our tobacco to a neighbor. Since Richard and I both worked away from the farm, there just wasn't enough time to strip the tobacco and get it ready for sale. This way we still get a little money from the tobacco, but we don't have to work until midnight in the stripping room.

New equipment is always changing the way we farm. Dad got our first corn picker in 1941. It was a one-row picker that shucked the ears and pitched them into a wagon. What an improvement that was over picking by hand! The whole family worked long hours picking by hand in the "good old days." I remember always putting in a few hours working in the corn field when I got home from school. The family always hoped for clear weather during the October full moon because the moonlight allowed us to work after dark getting in the crop. Sometimes we would be in the field until 11 o'clock. That's why the October full moon is called the Harvest Moon.

Around 1946, just after the Second World War, we got our first combine. It cut and threshed wheat in one operation. It was called a combine because it combined the jobs that the binder and the threshing machine used to do. No longer did we have to follow the binder to shock the sheaves or wait for the threshing machine to arrive to thresh the grain. The combine did the work of a whole crew of people in one operation.

After we got the combine, we began to grow more wheat. That machine was so expensive we needed to have more use for it. Our neighbors, the Clines, were thinking of retiring from farming. We leased their land so we could grow more wheat and soybeans. That's the way we could justify buying the combine.

The soybean has saved many a family farm like ours. It came from Asia and was first grown in the United States around 1900. My daddy remembered when the first soybean crops were grown around here back in the 1930s. Some farmers began growing soybeans and cutting them for hay. They grew them because the plant adds nitrogen to the soil, which corn and tobacco need. Later on, a market developed for soybean oil, and the price began to rise. Today soybean oil is used for all sorts of products from margarine to candy.

The biggest change in farming in the 1950s was the coming of hybrid seeds. With the hybrid seeds we could plant much more corn. In the old days, we used a corn planter that planted a hill of corn every 36 inches in rows 36 inches apart. With hybrid corn, we plant every 8 inches with rows 32 inches apart. The new corn grows better, too. I remember how excited we were the first year we averaged 100 bushels per acre. Now, that amount would be considered a poor crop, but back then it was great! My old grandaddy was happy with 40 bushels per acre.

Now we have a new combine head so the combine becomes

a corn harvester as well. It can pick and shell the corn in one operation. The corn cobs get left behind in the field as mulch rather than taking up room in the grain bins. No longer do we have to shovel corn by hand into the crib. Now it is unloaded by electric augers into big grain bins.

We set up our own grain storage bins so we can dry our grain on the farm and hold it for the best price. The price is usually lower at harvest time when lots of farmers are selling grain. It gets higher later. We like to hold our grain for a higher price or sell on contract for future delivery. We have to do everything we can to make money, because our costs are so high.

Because of the new hybrid seeds and harvesting machines, we had to make lots of other changes. To grow the new seeds, we must use lots of chemical fertilizers. Weeds choke the combine during harvest, so we often have to use weed killers. We don't cultivate the corn any more. Weed control is all done with chemicals.

Modern farming is becoming expensive. Just to plant a crop of corn or beans, we have to buy fertilizer, herbicide, seeds, and fuel for the tractor, and we have to hire extra labor. If we have a flood or if a late freeze kills the young plants, we are in real trouble. But farming has always been a gamble. To be a farmer, we have to take risks with the weather each year just as our ancestors did.

All this investment pays off in the good years. Our corn yield is now about 125 bushels per acre, with some fields running as high as 140 bushels or more. The new technology helps us keep pace with the growing cost and the growing markets. We certainly could not feed the world's population using farming methods from a hundred years ago!

Now we have tractors with air-conditioned cabs and radios to stay in touch with the farm office, which is our house. Richard can plant more corn in an evening after he gets home from work than my grandaddy could plant in a day.

The new tractors are big and powerful, but we still love the old 1936 John Deere. Richard has restored it, and we still use it for little jobs. He really enjoys playing with it. He just regrets that we don't have the old Fordson. My family gave it to a scrap-metal drive during World War II along with some other old tools.

I'm glad that we gave the old things to the scrap drive. It helped us win the war. Still, I like to go to farm museums and look at the old tractors and other equipment. They bring back memories of my daddy and grandaddy. How impressed they would be with what we have today! They would be amazed by our computer and how we figure costs and profits by just calling up a computer program. Now that is really the "good modern days!"

We work hard at soil conservation on the farm. We have to take care of the land if future generations are to survive. We build ponds in our pastures to store water for our cattle and to prevent the soil from being washed away. We use chisel plows to break the ground while still protecting it from washouts during heavy rains. On some of our hilly land, we use no-till farming, which doesn't require plowing at all.

We are beginning to restore our woodland. Most of our pastures were woods in the old days. Now we are planting trees to help hold the soil and to act as windbreaks around our fields. Some of our neighbors think we are crazy because windbreaks reduce our crop land by a few rows as the trees get big. We think it will be worth it if it saves even one inch of topsoil from being washed away by rain or blown away by wind.

I like the old Native American proverb that says: "We did not inherit the land from our fathers. We hold it in trust for our children." This proverb has a special meaning for me now. Henry and Marjorie are expecting! Richard and I had about given up hope of becoming grandparents, with Henry being too busy to get married for so long and Debbie with her medical practice. But now we are going to have a grandchild.

Henry and Marjorie have been to the doctor and have just come home with the news. They are going to have a little boy. The eighth generation of our family will soon be living on The Home Place.

I wrote at the beginning that my wedding day was the happiest day of my life. I may have to change that. I believe that I could not possibly be happier than I am today. I just pray that my grandson will want to live here and farm this land. I hope he will treasure it as his forebears have for all these generations. It will always be his Home Place.

6

Sarah's Letter

The Home Place

June 14, 1994

My Darling Grandson,

The news of your birth came to us at about 3 a.m. this very morning. Your daddy called from the hospital to tell us of your arrival and said that your mommy was doing fine. They had first called us when they left home for the hospital at about 7 p.m. Your grandfather and I were so excited we couldn't sleep. We are so very glad that you are here safe and sound.

Your grandfather has gone to sleep. He has to get up to go to work in a little while. I am too excited to sleep, so I am writing you this letter. When I finish it, I will give it to your daddy. He can give it to you when your are 21 years old as a special birthday present. I am 65 now and will be 86 then, if I am still around.

When you come home from the hospital, you will be the eighth generation of the Boyd family to live on this land. Your great-great-great-great-great grandparents settled here in 1799. This land has been our life and our living ever since.

Thomas Jefferson Boyd was born here in 1800, as were his two sons, Joseph and Henry. You are named Joseph Henry Boyd Wines after them. Henry's son, Little Jeff, and his son, Joe Bob, were born here as well. My brothers and I were born in the hospital, as were your daddy and you. But we were all born to this land just as much as if we took out first breaths here. Your heritage is here. It is a heritage which all those who now rest in the burying ground on the hill behind the barn worked so hard to give you.

Our family has another great heritage. It is the stories written by your forebears telling of their lives and how they helped to build this farm. Your grandfather and I have decided to have all these stories made into a book for you. You can keep it and learn about those who came before you. Maybe I will put this letter in it, too.

These stories are about your family, yes, but they are also about this farm we call The Home Place. This farm is special because it is our family home and the home of those who came before us. It is important for every person to know who they are and where they came from. There is nothing more valuable than to know that you are loved and that you can love in return. For generations the Boyds and now the Wineses have loved this farm, this special place.

Even those who go away still keep this love, this sense of place in their hearts. Your great Uncle Billy moved back home when he retired, and your Aunt Debbie still thinks of this as home even though she has lived in California for many years. Their roots are as firmly planted in the soil of this old farm as the roots of the trees your grandfather worked so hard to grow.

We are lucky to have our tradition here in this place. We used to have family over in Simpson County. Your grandfather and I went there not long ago. The farm that they once owned has disappeared. Part of it is now a strip mall and a modern subdivision. The rest is part of someone else's farm. Some times we hear from cousins. They are scattered all over the country, and their home, their special place is gone, except in memory. They have lost something they will never recover or replace.

Our greatest dream is that you will want to keep the tradition, that you will stay on and maintain The Home Place as a working family farm. One thing is for sure; we are no longer "hicks from the sticks" just because we live on the farm. We have the latest computers and soon we'll hook up to the Internet with links to the entire world. We have a satellite dish that lets us see more than 60 TV channels. It's amazing to me to sit in our living room and watch a program that can be seen by millions of people around the world.

We also depend on the whole world for our lifestyle. The gasoline in our car comes from oil pumped from the ground in the Middle East, or Africa, or Latin America. The coffee we drink, the sugar we put in it, and the many fruits and vegetables we eat come to us as a part of a world economy. Our corn and soybeans are made into food and products that may end up anywhere in the world.

By the time you are 21, it will be the year 2015. You may be an engineer or a scientist or an author, yet you may be able to do your work right here rather than in an office in some city far away. Whether you stay here or go away, I hope you will always think of this farm as your home.

Farming has changed so much, I have no idea what it will be like by that time. But I am sure there will still be room for the well-run family farm.

One thing is for sure. Farming will still be an act of faith. We gamble our very survival on the forces of nature. We have faith that the rains will come when they are needed. We have faith that the seeds will sprout, the animals will multiply, and the laws of nature will continue to hold true. Each decade we risk drought, flood, and storm. We accept these risks as part of life.

We also have faith in our fellow men. Almost everything we own in our business sits here on the land and is pretty much unprotected. We must hold on to the belief that our animals, our crops, our equipment, and our buildings will not be harmed or stolen. We can't guard them all the time. We must believe that people are basically good, and that they will respect what is ours as we respect what is theirs.

Above all we must have faith in our family and in the power of love. When you read the stories your ancestors wrote, you will see that their very lives depended on love and cooperation. They and their families and neighbors had to work together. They had a sense of community that bound them. They looked out for one another, not for personal gain, but for the good of each and all. That community is the ultimate act of faith for farmers, or for anyone, it seems to me.

This is the world in which you will grow up here on The Home Place. It is not a world that you will see on the evening news on TV. It is a world which fewer and fewer people are lucky enough to experience. You will learn that we are not always in control of our world. We are dependent upon the forces of weather that city people see only as something which might ruin their golf game or slow their drive to work. We are richer for being aware of the beauty of the summer rains or the benefit of a heavy winter snowfall. These are the very forces of life itself.

You will learn that we must conserve what we have. We must protect the land and the water. We can't just cut down trees. We have to plant groves of new trees. We have to dispose of our waste products safely and carefully because to do otherwise threatens our whole way of life. You will owe this trust to your children just as your ancestors owed it to you. I can't understand how anyone can claim to love our beautiful state without trying to preserve its environment.

Most of all, I hope you will learn about your past. We are all products of those who came before us. Read the stories of your family, and they will help you appreciate even more the value of this good land. It has been nourished by the blood and sweat and tears of good men and women. Treasure this heritage, little Joseph Henry, that you may pass it on to the generations that will come after you.

Most of all, your grandfather and I hope and pray that you will treasure each day and the beauty it brings you. Take time in your life to enjoy what you have.

Keep in your mind what your ancestor, Thomas Jefferson Boyd, wrote nearly two hundred years ago: "I truly believe that there is no greater place than where I live and no more beautiful sight than sunset on the Green River."

Your loving grandmother,

Sarah Boyd Wines

About the Author

Lee A. Dew retired from Kentucky Wesleyan College in 1994 after teaching history for nearly 40 years. He holds degrees from the University of Arkansas, Kansas State, and Louisiana State.

He is the author of 10 published books and more than 50 articles, many of which deal with issues surrounding agriculture.

A member of the Kentucky Humanities Council's Speakers Bureau, he gives talks throughout the Commonwealth on the subject of Kentucky barbecue and "Agriculture: Kentucky's Least-Known Resource."

He is the father of three grown children. His wife, Aloma W. Dew, is also a historian and serves as chairperson of the Kentucky Environmental Quality Commission.